The Avatar of
a Cross Check

The Avatar of a Cross Check

First Edition

BY

Nur Aifiah Binti Ibrahim

Published in India by Prowess Publishing,
GJ Complex, Thadikara Swamy Koil St, Alandur,
Chennai, Tamil Nadu 600016

ISBN: 978-1-5457-6315-5

Library of Congress Cataloging in Publication

Table of Contents

A Philosopher's Guide

A pebble of stone placed on a pond produced overlapping ripples. The rustling wind behind the garden shows that the night is hefty. The sudden change in weather and the telecommunication teleportation is out of order. The security guard in the cockpit was busy eating doughnuts. They missed a snapshot of a samurai passing through in front of the surveillance camera. Before this, their eyes were glued to the TV screen without realising the gear nut was out of sight. The escapee, Joe tries his best to use his wittiness in having a spray of a formula to pass through the lasers. He also wore a cool vest, a man of action who even studied these moves on television. He quickly grabs the nut which is priceless for his next invasion. He even won an auction to have a blueprint for his latest project of sabotaging a bakery near his hometown.

Then, his sidekick, Julian spent his time on building blocks and did his homework to assist Joe with his escapism. He is very loyal and from time to time he will remind Joe to stay low. Both of them were known for their closeness and cleverness. They have the same opponent, Aaron who always looked up to them for no reason. He noticed their tiredness and the dark circles under their eyes which showed they were up to something. Sooner or later, Aaron continues with his project. He sat in a living room and played a musical tune. The moment he left the room he turned on the radio and noticed his father's company in a challenging state.

He even went to his father's office to look at his father's eyes and be more open with him. His father appreciates his worthiness and tells him to run the business with him. It is a newspaper company where he works for a living and shares stories with the people. He builds up his character and generosity. On the way back home he is just a simple guy. At work, he is the superhero. There is a suspicious guy named Tim living across the road. He even invited Aaron to his house and noticed the frustration on his grinning face. Tim turned out to be a health problem and Aaron spent his investment by giving hope and non-stop overflowing of caretaking him at home. He is trying to fix things but people keep pushing him away because of the incident.

He built a tower out of a deck of cards until it tumbled down. He is always with his father until he decides to move to another town where he first sees Kevin, a boy who keeps greeting him. Their bonding is very close and they are brothers. He builds a tree house for climbing and a hammock by the pool. He accompanies Kevin to the bus school. As soon as the bus arrived, street performers and dancers were ready for a parade. There is a food court at the entrance of the hall.

In a different house vibe, building a camping site, and celebrating my new love for home. There are also television displays and a go-kart in the backyard, Kevin. Aaron also invited the Wongs for a home-cooked dinner. I had never seen such a happy family vibe around them only if Aaron be with them. Aaron shared the same interests as them. The record breaker for holding his breath too long underwater is Mr. Wong himself. He even posted his picture of the diving site on the site of the cliff. There were also cable cars towering uphill and a Cafe at a nearby restaurant.

As Aaron resembles a cape crusader, the boy dreams of a different action figure. All they did was spend time together, swiping each other's turnovers to know how it feels like to ride in a levitated bedroom. They both are family man which and foremost look after their families. They also watched an anime movie that emphasises family values. What is love? All they know about is taking the time to travel on a train and another ballistic ride to have fun hopping on a Jurassic Park boat even to the wildest imagination. The child always remembers his embrace and smiling-looking eyes to divert himself from the darkest moment. It is not a red carpet moment but everything that he does is mirrored. To prepare for a remembrance in a Crystal ball infused with button modes and sensories for the record of his happiness level.

They practiced preparing dinner on the table and grabbing him by the arm to catch up on the stairs and cross the roads. Every time, Kevin got back from his class, his parents playfully invited him over to dinner and more munchies on the silver screen at their home theater. They are whimsical and they even have family gatherings for playtime, such as moulding clays, family petting zoos, and planning to build a new home for their hamsters and guinea pigs. For every Christmas and family occasion, we planned on a theme between the breaks, and there was something caught in between as Kevin is a bit of an observant, and his curiosity is boundless. He loves to spend his time on the laptop to look up his social media and communicate with his hamsters for more feeders.

Cultural Adversity

They suddenly by a nearby petrol station and saw something mysterious coming out of the shrubs and bushes by the side of the long road. There seems to be a group of villagers who have been practicing their postures to clear away the sorghums. Leaving his Captain America behind, Aaron kept him in his memories. Suddenly, Mother screamed for an eerie-looking hometown and an abandoned tractor parked in front of the old restaurant. It gives the rustic feeling of living in a lifeless yet so vast desert of hope. They kept away their worries and uneasiness in focusing on others. They avoid their very best from becoming the talk of the town. They have been greeted by charming friendly neighbours who would always share a piece of baguette out on the way from the French pastries nearby. They repay his generosity by making guacamole and enchiladas for their favourite family snack. Every night Kevin will go up to his laptop for more words of wisdom and continuous support from his admirable, Aaron.

Aaron seems to be pleased with his gladness and blistering of gems keeping him in awe every other day.

He would not let himself be sad again and do what it takes to challenge the human mind in becoming an adult with the thoughtless act of being left with things let alone there is no one to turn to. That is so not true compared to those who are used to the regimen of a military camp that keeps their eyes on safety and health concerns for the community. However, their jobs did not stop there as they were those who played it manipulatively by attacking others and sticking their noses into power and domination. That is the first thing people would do is to not get involved and head down to other peaceful areas of the countryside home to nature where people appreciate the true being and manage their healing of stressful life and other stimulants for panicking disorders.

Depending on the situation that they were in. They put on a tent before going into the suburbs for their convenience in the meantime. They went up to a store and boiled themselves some Ramen and other sandwiches just to keep them well-fed. They are not afraid of taking chances and are brave when handed their money over the counter. They wished they could see more lively faces and accommodate the areas under the supervision of the American highly qualified security agents. The father even laughs himself out at the thought of putting on an act just to move them out of town. However, Father always makes sense of the situation and calms them down not picturing anything more unusual and unbearable to witness with. Father shoved us over not to be so paranoid and alarming for that will be a pressure cooker for them all.

The blistering wind and an open space to look at the stars in the sky. It seems to have replaced the room where Kevin spends most of his time talking to the fluffies. They can be adorable but sensible in giving him the warmth of graceful tiny hands placed upon his hand. His heart is soft and delicate from what he had watched Brave the movie portrays a lady but even for boys she is a heroic figure for not escaping what is in front but appreciating the beauty and miscellaneous individuals and beings that they can ever be. As a child people are expected to listen to them but they are continuously in a guessing game and constrained by the rules. There is no freedom for them to voice out even on a rare occasion to bring up some mature stories and use them to go against their evil wills. He always wears a blazer as if he was an announcer on a stage. He even has to keep all his future endeavors and endless thoughts in being a responsible and charismatic superhero of his Mother and Father.

He imagined that they were hamsters standing line by line represented by the distinct colours of ribbons. They went up to a man-built tree house and communicated among them in a new meeting every day. Such a simple philosophy and game they put them in. What matters is now to build a water cycles in watering the plants or picking up the seeds from the bag full of sunflower seeds. They cannot expect a hamster to run on a treadmill to prove their productivity and masculine act of being athletic. If they are sick they will make themselves of a mattress and blanket for their families' shade. They even warm themselves up and keep on warning each other to keep away from the home cage.

Another story is on pessimistic world. Like a chaotic world, when there is not enough food to eat. They loved to be in a backyard to search for a good food source. They are very good at finding lost and found items underground. They even broke a nail while digging to show their heroic attempts to save a rabbit after being caught on a net near a stream. They can break the knots by biting them with a sharpened fang. They chased away humans in their own way. They are in the form of soldiers. The community understands their fight and makes a peace deal by signing the acorn exchange deal. Farmers are worried about their dominant and colonial act of retrieving what is theirs in the hands of their Chief. The Chief, in the end, put down his weapon of sticks and catapults of pebbles for more respect of their human friends. They even have a financial education and become more literate and absorbed in their barter system.

3

Family Investment

There is a dinosaur parade in New York. Kevin met the celebrity chefs and night watchers are there also for fine dining. The clock tower suddenly alarmed near them. They feel startled and urgent about another movie while watching at the cinema. Look, there is a cowboy who lives in an old town and confesses his love for a beautiful and elegant lady who looks him in the eye and switches roles as she grabs him and pulls the trigger to aim at their nemesis for their greed in love. Kevin holds his popcorn as it almost falls to the ground. Mother whines as the Father passes over the Soda water. They expected the scene to be touching and loving, instead, it turned into an action movie. As the film ends, the cowboy recites the old county sheriff as he leans by the horse's stand.

Kevin learned that the old county deserves more natural resources than just blinking oil. Mother even commented about the Lady who is so heroic that she teared up after listening to the sorrowful sonnet that rested upon her sleeves. Amusingly, Mother wanted to copy her Western clothing so Father went to a clothing brand store to have them wearing the Winter's edition. It sounded more compelling as it resembled the cowboy who even had a strong bearded face. However, the atmosphere in the hometown was filled with haystacks and blown-off dusty wind covering up the space. In Kevin's space, there are orbital orders and intersection points of meeting the alignment of the stars. He even imagined the Heavens where he best put upon him. That is the law he could not get enough of.

The librarians did not look at him as another boy just curious with small hands. However, Aaron's trainer tells him otherwise. He is ready to be a man even at such a young age. Kevin does not need to follow Aaron's orders and instructions to feel commanded all the time. The up and down stacks featured in the computer monitor do not indicate his selfish motives and his purity shows the way into Aaron's life of a different premonition. The cyclist even holds the handlebars to steer the wheel down the road by feeling the adrenaline when protecting and reaching for their hands in balancing and letting the body move aerodynamically according to the law of curvature.

Kevin invented his own game of gestures and the way he teaches Grandfather when reading a newspaper, he even feels happier than ever. Grandfather is always there to listen and witness his precision in reading and writing. By writing, he is like a marketeer and sticks his head up knowing that he is almost finished with the sentences and is literate on various topics. They gave the world to Kevin and Mother and Father respected his working field. Aaron imagines himself as the boss. Something he is deprived of. What Aaron did was monitor his progress instead of looking at the charts. Without a hidden agenda, he just kept silent and was afraid not to mentor him up close. There are phases and stages, these terms are not in his dictionary and dashboard.

They often keep their hidden agenda out of sight but get caught. From their weary actions and easy-to-catch their wrongful actions, Aaron is becoming more aware of not involving Kevin and the professionalism in his field should not be of his concern. He does not win by an argument and hurtful comments. However, God is always by his side. Aaron also wanted to weigh in on the odds of having unwanted intentions as he kept on crying and worrying until he could make up his mind. They both share as the world spins around like in the hall of mirrors. There are too many incidents and shout outs to have a definite moment for clarification. However, one day Kevin feels strange and lets himself fall into the arms of Aaron.

He chuckles as there are no more action movies but Disney movies instead. Aaron did not stop him but reminded him about the fluffiness of the world of marshmallows. Their cuteness and adorableness could not get enough of them. Kevin even dreamed of getting them home and expanding their backyard. By not keeping Kevin under his magnifying glass. He shows his love and affection by keeping him feeling happy and motivated. However, he didn't realise his reactions got worse as he observed his Grandfather's health charts. He thought to himself that he had to endure the sadness and keep on living. He learned to pick up the mess and help organize room stuff that keeps on disorganised in the living room. He also had a foldable table and practiced adjusting his postures so he could reach the laptop screen to continue writing of his free will.

With his determination and endless battles with the numbers, he suddenly has imaginative numbers not to be restricted by the standard Mathematics workflow and off the grid. He was also inspired by the authors and co-authors of Physics and how they broke the rules and defended their theses to get on with the proposed ideas. They are not made-up theories. To solve a logical problem, there is a sequential and interconnected world of related bonds of chemicals that have not been explained. It is not a literate name to call it articulate, but more of an abstract and iterative process. He is so computerised and people are afraid of those things like how the Mayans built their sky labs to be more meticulous in their predictions.

They built pyramids and Kevin more to building a sandwich club and started to boil the pasta and make it into a spaghetti meatball. They thought that having the food on the table had already made them Western, but Kevin's idea is still beyond the Universe. What he did was to make sure the living room had always been his. One of the topics chosen is the 3-D revolutionary shapes. He only uses his trial and error when varying the angles, lengths, and limits to challenge the infinity loops, hyperbolas, and ellipsoids. After watching Bloomberg,

Aaron is interested in getting the deal right but does not think of enough patterns when making a share.

Until he saw Kevin's playing with numbers. He reverses his psychology and becomes more equipped with numbers. He went to a local farming market and saw them counting and weighing the whole time, but most people know the best option is to be more intuitive and learn by their instincts. For instance, to him, labour is nothing but making you feel occupied and productive, the whole process of it. Rather than looking at bulleted points and acting in a system. It is not burnout but he rather burns all of these negative thoughts and puts them into his measurements for his pleasure in seeking happiness for his loved ones. It is not the care that counts, and so is the efforts that spill through the assorted beans. That kind of imagery itself did not express the mood of trying but more to staying composure for a steady state.

4

Family Retreat

They went to a bookstore and there they found all the related reading materials that they could find in cooking until knitting. These household chores that they wanted to do so much are also limited. They even experimented with the social circle they implemented to have a fair attention and deep interest in fighting for justice. They even met a social network expert, Prof. Nathan from Oxford University. According to Prof. Nathan, studying human behaviour is not a good sign if they start with a frown and eye glaring.

Eye glaring is a way to show that you are stared down and to expect a different reaction from that person is impossible. They cannot look away and dodge out their faces. When the person with a more prepared position to present their content of writing. They are more with words in writing and seeking advice for their monotonous tone to set in together with the execution. Even a cat can sense her intentions and walk away from it. By making it more repulsive, she tries to make herself more flattering and available for social reasons.

Aaron and Kevin explain further the situation that they are in welcoming others is very well adapted. According to Prof. Nathan, adaptation is not to brag about and before they make themselves into the circle and allow themselves to reach by themselves, they cannot even feel themselves. The minor problem is that when other people understand you but don't mind what the person is facing can also be intimidated and the rudeness makes other people feel like they have to accept the fact that they are being used. They are coming back for more. Even Prof Nathan cannot reason out the destructible behaviour and counterattacks.

At home, Aaron and Kevin even greet and fit into a hole for more interactive activities and attractions to visit. It is all set even if not taking a roller coaster ride or other extreme rides. It is a free ride but when it comes to Cats they are all over. They try to understand the existence and are tempted to see them do the body flip and curling-like flexibility of the body. Aaron finishes his sketch by outlining a feline species, the Cat. Then, Kevin's colour features and visuals try to suit the colours according to the background.

They even make way for cats to walk. Catwalk is the science of studying the walk and posture that no people ever wanted but is what British people do without slouching and leaning back that much. However, the stiffness of those postures breaks your bones and no one is to blame for the soft muscle that was not put into use. How to keep their family not under surveillance and continue with a serious interest in entertaining themselves. From the gate to the backyard. They are not obsessed but concerned about social security problems. Not by the wealth they possess but by their well-being as if they walking down the Alley at night. The kind of social endorsement and third parties that could not even be trusted they have to use a different signature and faulty pen just to fool them.

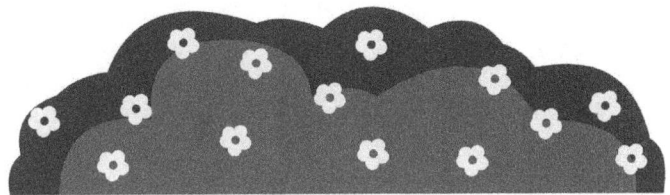

5

A Tree By The Train

The seed of knowledge has always been standardised and changing from a long time ago. The teacher is Mother. Why Kevin could not have both a Mother and Father? Aaron could not explain it but Kevin figured it out all day and all night just to be with them. Grandfather and Aaron acknowledge him to think for himself. From a boy to another boy. It takes ages to have them written in a record. In Korea, they watched a lady in the palace keep on addressing Her Majesty as the Mother of the Nation. She even stood up for her people when facing the era in which ladies did not belong in a palace kitchen to serve them goodness.

People look at a lady as if she already made up for the role. Why didn't they respect her? The best they could do was to greet them. It is the custom and the bereavement that people do not want to bear. It can be traumatic and shocking to have to accept it as a personal excuse to allow more to come. However, so elegant and independent, up to the point of crushing others is not what they getting at but the disappointment that they cover for social well-being. The timeline for it to stay is too short and it is not everlasting since there are generations of ladies who are more profound but just as Prof. Nathan pointed out it is another age of labelling and naming characters to keep on debating society what is the best trait or not. What is the best status and what is wrong in being an innocent person?

While riding in a speedy and aerodynamic shape like a plane magnetically connected to the trail. They felt as if floating in the air with nothing to hold onto. Kevin already imagined himself being in an overcrowded train full of cartoon figures and animated series to lighten the mood in an old countryside. Spend time bickering and love to shout out commanding words to make themselves feel relieved and out of gesture. Be careful of the weather and neighbours, they are always the coincidental themes to go out with. They even come across a strained lady before and they have been warned about the exposure of up closures that have been put upon their unnecessary visionaries.

Not by wanting to come down by the school even parked in front of the field. Kevin understands the atmosphere and pressure of being inside a classroom. However, Kevin is an intelligent boy scout and Aaron loves to be part of his vision and outgoing outdoor projects. Grandfather is always in their minds. Grandfather even kept silent about his health condition. However, they noticed the sudden changes in his meal and napping time. They even went to a bookstore to buy a magazine which they subscribed monthly. He refused to go to the health department but to stay at home and enjoy watching movies. They gave him time for his moment in relaxing mode.

There is a moment in his life to say no to youngsters nowadays.

They keep on changing weather and they don't even know when to stay calm and think more rationally. However, as Aaron and Kevin came into his life he felt more open and a part of his Universe came into a navigating system where they had more to explore. He even pushed away people from coming into the Observatory room where he kept all the stargazing equipment and tools for measuring the speed and orbital impact of the blown-up stars scattered across the galaxy in a distance. Rather than watching meteorology, Grandfather is a good reading man as he is into the space and galaxy mischievous thing to handle and could not get enough of. Aaron was in the other room fixing things and fitting the puzzle pieces together.

Kevin is still studying the closet and dressing room which expanded as he grew up one day. He listens to his Mother and Father's advice when he is calm or needs their guidance during the Winter season. On the train trip, they even went to a small town library. They watch on the news that Winter is coming and get ready with snow shovels and thick boots when going out. Aaron worries about the fact that Kevin is by his side the whole time. He decided to bring him along for a Grandfather's visit. All the time he is all about schoolwork and projects. Pupils surrounded him like there was no other than interrupting his knowledge skills and hand craftsmanship. He keeps on finishing his shoe rack in the working lab to make sure all the nuts and bolts are in place.

He built his inventions, but he only managed to draw them on a blueprint. He went through a lot lately putting himself in his shoes. He admires an inventor named Prof. George who assisted him with his next project of saving a herd of buffaloes on a farm.

At first, Kevin made an acquaintance with Lucas, the buffalo with a yellow ribbon on his neck. Instead of ordering another batch of full green grasses, he even fed them the fresh ones he planted on his own. Not to forget his family hamster who would always greet him every morning to have their light feet on track. Then, he went out and fetched a pail to water the plants. He bravely being trained by a friendly farmer named Papa Sam who draws the buffalo's attention by bringing the wonder stick to lead them in line according to a Lady thesis, the opening of the lad will make sure their heads will turn in a certain rotation for the remote sensors to be alerted by the detectable part of their brains in having some adjustment to allow them to get inside of the barn. Therefore, there is no force to be implied in that theory as it is the safest and best thesis they have ever read for centuries.

6

An Indian Performer

There is a bit of Asian fusion as well. One day, they met an Indian performer in a lively concert. The Bollywood theme did not go with the music flow in their lives. Aaron and Kevin are enthusiasts in their reading culture and eating their authentic taste in paneer and puree. In Western, they pronounce it as puree, which is a liquefied and starchy looking appetizer that rhymes with a polenta dish. The mashed potato and the carrot's crunchy texture has a light taste and is up to my appetite. They are even overblown by the spiciness and the tanginess of the lime is overpowering by the herbs and spices.

In India, anything is possible. They are withdrawn by their spiritual life and culture. They are more fluent in speaking and very diligent in their work. They go for respecting other cultures, but are more English-like in the evening tea and crumpets. Aaron and Kevin accepted as it was. From what they observe, they are not into Korean waves and other Asian tantrums. In their makeup line, they have their beauty essences and natural organic products, such as turmeric, that go well with lemon juice, which are naturally complex for the skin. How much they value family and health. Their earthy responses even revive the Earth's natural core to the trees breathing within the roots. They didn't experience a martial art to go with the natural defenses when attacking someone.

Music is not something to be proud of. Listing names and charts are by recording labels that are signed and owned by the pioneers themselves. The Titanic and the gigantic era of ruling is just like in the United Kingdom. Who is the founder but to put himself or herself in the muse by what they had provoked and salvaged, destroyed by the out of tune? Aaron himself, as the music producer, learned that tribal rhythm and Western oppressive acts in an opera were even intimidated by the false accusation and red lips and pale skin of an Opera mask man to lead his role. Not being played by others to gain more of themselves, but to know the masking effect always on the lure of the streets.

However, the new generation is not a societal paradigm but the next movers into another nomad and living mechanism to movie stompers and yes, the Korean wave seems to do their own thing. They keep on learning and innovating music for their companionship, and they are always in the trend and not out of tune. It is not up to them but their music exits the trends and is played on their music recordings endlessly. Kevin learned how to speak Korean and respects Indian culturalism. However, the way they studied at the airport was not to look at other people's faces in a friendly manner and put up a steady face. However, it is hard to read people's faces in times of facing the community and the education centres. They even forgave them for being brave in class to be in a line of examination study to fulfill their targeted achievement and having a good score is what started the whole monkey fest.

Sometimes, Kevin has to respect their music interlude to beat around the bush. All they know is to pick a broom and jet-lagged from an international private jet. They thought of it as a depiction and classroom resonance, no need for further action taken under a school ruling. They went on and on until Kevin learned to adjust to the environment and know their bags and tricks. There is a cultural diversion overlooking the sea and the air for a more breathtaking view.

They have been up the hill and looking to recite a musical expression from the drops of rain to the tinted glass on the window. Mother and Father would cling to the glass. The tunes are like in the music of their hands. Steady hands should do the trick. The music therapy plays in a ting tune creating a calm and relaxing vibe to accompany the roomy space in between. Aaron shares his guitar tuning and keyboards on a different note. Kevin even had the intention of exploring music in his outperforming arts. He knew all about the materials and leather making of cow skin on the drums to create a strong thumping and repetitive musical traditional beating of the system.

They even went for a jukebox and other tuning musical instruments to study the morphological and other taxonomies of botanicals. From sharp edges of leaves to longer vines that channel through the vibrating and reflective sound on the surface of the plant, can replace the tranquility of the early bird stand. In earlier days, they requested and became more ecological by wearing hats out of fruit baskets to be more creative—tomatoes and other vegetable seeds when catapulted against a wooden plank and board to have a smash hit. Hardened objects refrain from the ancient musical bands as they can be playful tools for hitting others. Without harming them, they have their circles and to be a member of a pack, they must be pleased and mastered at their greatest attempt. Some are going solo and these global orchestras have stirred their hearts and miming is the way of showing it. However, overplaying it causes the act to be more expressive and delivered by a sketching book.

A fun time together equals the time for the launching of their new project. By looking out the window, he found himself in a garage. He put in his effort to carve a flower-engraved pattern onto a wooden plank to test his craftsmanship. Before this, he even went to an aquarium where there were new species of fish that had been introduced, and the new way of feeding and breeding them also made them participate in the crowd. There are ornamental fishes in the aquarium and decorative fish tanks that have to face a predatory species. Within seconds, they have their meal and look for a shelter for not sharing it.

Then, they headed to a Dessert place where they found themselves for a treat. They enjoyed a nice ice shaving by the beach while watching dolphins and penguins. There is so much to know about their daily activities, since dolphins, the adorable and more humanistic, seem to have a bad side of it for attacking humans on a rare occasion. In the first place, Kevin never wanted to be there and witness the incident. In reality, sharks are more predatory, and their sharp teeth tell it all. There is a bit of Science going on, and explaining to children can be a fun experience to have, and they went for another sightseeing and made it to the gift store.

They bought a cushion and other stationery to give them to Grandfather, Mother, and Father. Mother hugged Kevin for giving her one of the best gifts she ever had after winning his heart to go on a Jeep trip to the Night Zoo. The horticulture is put in live-action to challenge the climate by making the open space in the jungle even more breathable. However, the streamlining of flower buds and other vineyards really can be eye-popping for the flower panels to be in an assembly line. After placing them in an igloo structure, the Dome of Hall was even served with a welcoming herbal tea and scrumptious cakes and pastries to go with the flower event. From that time, engineers also built a water fountain and provided a living space for them to engage with. Not provided with the manual, there is an instinct to prompt design in pumping and filtering the water at the same time.

Certain naturalists and geologists fasten up the process, but through several attempts at in-depth cultivation and seismological planting activities, they drag the off-stream from piling up the stacks to relinquish it from the thorns and spikes thrown from the pop-up of flowers. They went on a business trip to Australia, the land of the outback, to accentuate the modern-day city lights and bridges to the field of gusting winds. A different environment and interpretation of the horticulturist that they are practicing. They even have a stop sign for the seasonal crustaceans to pass along the coast. As a protector, they write on a chalkboard for the ideas to come and blend in. They even watched the seals and sea lions go head to head for their playtime and chase their children in the open space for them to sleep and cuddle. That is the moment when they spotted an opportunity to commemorate the natural diversity and to showcase it in a different populated urban space.

7

Wind Blowing Farm Field

Kevin let his imagination run wild by having his friends on board the new road vehicle, gardening inside and outside the farming zone. He would not want his lunch to go away without having a taco meal with guacamole dressing on the salad. They thirst for another ongoing project to practice an eco-friendly support to the environment and community. They were overblown by the fact that the lack of electricity and the power mill seems to take time in reaching the whole power hubs placed in each one of the houses. Kevin grabs Aaron by the shoulder to begin their first experience in testing over the current water in a storage tank and the overflowed river that generates the quartz and the discovery of the Loch Ness monster. Their amazement of digging a tunnel to make the wiring sure takes time, having to be stranded in a desert of oasis filled with Earth cracking and the mountain of sand to slide over. Their endless journey challenges them to fix and rewire the whole place. Imagine a land full of ice and glaciers, to a dry out land which represents two different climates along the road.

The water temperature in the cooler state by the divers for the corals and seaweeds to uncover the hidden Quartz. To understand the living, they even climbed the tea plantation nearby for a more shallow water. Their reflections are shown up on the surface. Out in a clear land, they cut the grass and decided to do more planting and vegetation. However, they never left the bookkeeper off hand, instead they even sought assistance from local farmers to have the fresh produce and richness of the blackcurrant juice. The trail never ends, overlooking the mountains with a hook movable ride facing across the hidden fortress set by the clear field of woods. They went on and on to reach the barren land filled with astrolabs, which functioned as the measurements and calculative stacks of the crystallised shards, line by line to have a contact with the time and space.

They forsake the living in returning to the nature. They are on a nationwide discovery for the rightful owners of the underprivileged and moving mountains. Kevin went on a water slide as Aaron took another exit of the trail to await his arrival. The species of monkeys and chimpanzees are very entertaining by the rubbing of their chests and the fruit bunch full of bananas. The eating of fruits is a kind of pulpy and burst of tanginess and fruitiness flavours in different tropical flavours to choose from. There is even a Monkey bar to enjoy for the selective choices over different sauces to dip the shrimps and calamari. They even went to the pouring rain to place their shiny boots on the puddle of water. The clock tower shows already past 9 in the night for the crows and owls to set on the line wires placed on top of the rooftops and open buildings. They went in for a good night's sleep to have another age of clues and ancient studies on the global map.

They went in for another glass of blueberry and red berry juice to have it with the crunchiness of the carrots. Locals are advised to enjoy the batch of carrots to eliminate the feeling of nausea and vomiting and keep themselves on a bright side for the new day. Geographically, the streets are on the verge of the new day and welcoming for the new food industry in craving for more Italian pestos and zucchini strips. They ordered the eggplants stuffed with melted cheese and chilli flakes to have a balanced flavour with the hint of sage enhancing the fragrance of the dish. There is a sudden change in the weather, which brought the clouds together, and the frictionless air can be charged with the ions to unleash the thundering sound of the clouds and booming sound that comes all over the quiet day. Never be so intrigued by the social networks that promise fake hopes to calm the whole city with the incident of losing electrical power in the land of the centre monument.

They have gone through the old roads for the Egyptian of the Abu Simbel. From there, the megalithic structure deserves a more historical description and remarks for the new era to vibe so different from the ancient ruins. The train trail is the best environment for seeking another exciting jump off from a cliff to be directly rerouted into the underwater sea. Kevin gave a thought over the top of the land to the tunnels of widened story on cultural and urban legends that explain the intriguing phenomena to have its endless encounters. Suddenly, the jellyfishes are popping up on the water surface, electrifying and feeling as aquatic as possible. The landlord of the place gives a hidden seeking for more clues to uncover the realness of the whole locomotion over the local news for the Loch Ness monster.

They did not do much about it, but even accepted their presence as it is floating on the sea of the mysterious tales. They referred to an ocean discoverer diving in the special tank made of glass flasks and seats with buttons placed even on the armrest. The captain takes on the voyage by pressing the button of vibrating the stand beneath the explorer tank as they sat behind the open gauge. The captain levered down and pulled down the wire on the boat to make sure it was lifted, lowered down into the gap and deep holes of the Belitz. There is another mystical lake found underneath the sea, for the methane and nitrogen to bubble up beneath the surface before the air bubbles are produced. They are immersed by the breathtaking aquarium sight even though they had it on shore. Many have theorised the movement of water to the birth of a living organism that set a sail off shore for its survival on the foreign land.

Aaron's kept himself a stone and ores resembled the old age of fossils to have carbon prints all over it. The overnight submerging of the aquatic plants to other greenery. Kevin's uplifted spirit brings back to nature to have a live worm in a pail full of soil and earthworm. He released the worm into the Earth soil for more nutrient uptake in the inverted land. The surroundings play a key role in unlocking the truth behind the mechanical story of using a water generator to have it unearth the river stream and catch the attention of other chipmunk-looking beavers to have it on check. His wisdom took off by the neck tie he wore to school. The school project involved an ancient build-off prototype so that every story behind the walls unfolds the unsettling arguments and debates to fit in a pothole.

8

A Monumental Beginning

They managed to stumble across the colours of the sands of sand forming the patterns and the rainbow colours of minerals forming on their steps, made their way to the nearby restaurant. The colourful graffiti even paved their way for their ongoing taste journey across the city. The wooden tables and chairs were wiped very clean and neat as they put on a special solution to have a woody smell, sat by the fiery chimney. Their first course is the roasted chicken braised in a pot full of vegetable stock. The juicy flavours coming out from the steamer caught their eyes on the burning charcoal of an Indonesian snack food called Otak-Otak. The symphony of flavours continues with the next course for dessert. They have filled in the hollow of a crusted Cannolis with silky smooth flavours of chocolate and strawberries.

The waiter turned on the jukebox for the more chilling tune to commemorate with the jazzy feel of cozy around the woodfire spot. The South Carolina inward buildings caught everybody's attention as their woke celebrities have blurred down the streets for something more shiny and silver like aerodynamic shaped vehicle which wanders across the street. They stopped by the local stores to grab something to go, beholding the tacos and sandwiches in a delightful and more stacks of flavours for different textures of sliciness and spiciness of the meat to the crunching sound of the small cut vegetables. They go on for the sleepiness in a bluish and purplish colour of the shaving ice for more intense flavours of the frostbite. Kevin imagined the stainless steel with a few holes all over it to strain off the lushiness of the lettuce wraps and the sweet and sour flavours of the mixed formula sauce.

The whole bank in a quiet city had a tagging for marketing indexes to have a wavering and inflatable banners to overflow across the street. They even went to see the brokers and financial advisors took on a live action in having a labour turnover to support more on the economy growth. By clicking on the trend analysis and monetary charts, they played on darts and swapped with the tic tac toe for another puzzlement on the liquidity of money management. Interesting facts of the outgrowth of the mushrooms and popping cherries scattered in the land of building concretes for another town planning. Their average hours of unbeatable outbreak, which get them beefed up with the outstanding counts of money outrageous. Their economic empowerment, plus the whole aggravating processes, foretold another story of a merchant who carried the food cart, and the relaxing hours also become more productive with the time management being the key for more success to come.

There is so much life to find something new. Behind the wilderness of a boy, Kevin sets in a new time frame where he had his compass and notepads for another marking of the new beginning. He even added a facet into his list of jewelry to accessories his treasure chest of having the time of his life. There is no by far any chance that he wanted more for Aaron than to have extra attention to self-realisation over something invaluable than his personal feelings and agitations of being with someone you barely knows. He grabs a bunch of fruits and vegetables to have them on the tablecloth for more snacking. After completing the light snack, they happened to see a seesaw and an empty pool by a nearby house. The house is said to belong to a faithful owner of the Bears, a varsity blues of a township college. In honouring their accomplishments in the written names of the Billboard chart of a city light.

Aaron also stopped by his studio apartment to do some follow up on his current job of new postings. The structural and monumental contributions seem to be outstanding as his name is all over the place. Kevin could not have been so proud of his achievement and still supports his ongoing progress for the next project in line. Some are randomly visited to one of his memorable architecture, and some keep on taking pictures to have a livelier society of the night and day. The never-ending story makes sure that the afterlife is more adaptable and immersed in the new urban, like-futuristic kind of structure. He paid attention to the details and has yet to survive the business hurdles to jump into other product management for the design and innovation sector.

Kevin, as usual, put on his helmet and knee pads to have an adventure of his own at school. He explores the outer environment and avoids becoming more doubtful and uncontrollable to show his skillful learning. The stages of development can be very steep with many new technical and observational learning to climb from. He shares his gift of thoughts with his family and Aaron to have an overnight stay up assignments accompanied by his hot English tea and crumpets full of pastries spread with jam and honey. He came forward in front of the class to prove the theorem in challenging the law of momentum. The implacable impact of the release and triggered mind is to set it in a free zone by not allowing others by putting his heart out for an artful design.

9

The Convincing Truth

They have ended their conversation most profoundly. Aaron puts on a straw hat with a ring of flowers around it. He is overtaken by the hotel basement, politely greeted by the locals. He enjoys every moment of it. He holds a glass of pineapple juice with an umbrella on it. He did not expect a fan from his old hometown to come and greet him by the counter. There is a convincing truth that the fan could be his old friend or old colleague. What a small world. There is not much to do in the lonely hours. He went on a short trip accompanied by his assistant, Jonathan. Jonathan went on and on by sharing personal experience in extreme weather forecasting. He overheard about a new exotic place where he could explore his latest invention to impress Kevin. His inner thoughts brought up his smart deal with the other educational school. He welcomes new students from the kindergarten tree house team to the adulthood of masterful skills.

He brings about the education in front of Jonathan as the topic is serious. He told Kevin about his favourite eating place for peanut butter and jelly. He is a fit master guru in stretching poses and limb movement. He even went for aqua training for the next empty schedule, authoritatively knowing that his business proposals need to be checked. He even does the gardening himself and shares it with his local produce. They urged them to make it in front of the department chairs by sharing their untold stories and let the Grandfather know what he is made of. Silicon Valley and other brokers' job employment has business tenders to attend to as well.

They spent countless hours trying to have a maze and tic tac toe on the puzzle that they left for their pre-openings over a workshop to pass over from one generation to another. All they care about is the land that they found mysterious to handle. Kevin extended his neck and managed to take a glimpse at the painting that he always wanted to share with Aaron. Then, they kept their things away as the discussion forum had already ended, and they headed to the room which they finally made for their future embankments. Their endless efforts of searching and guessing keep the waiting time in the wormhole for another ancient discovery. There is nothing on board at the moment for their bear fruit journey to another region called Alaska. The End.

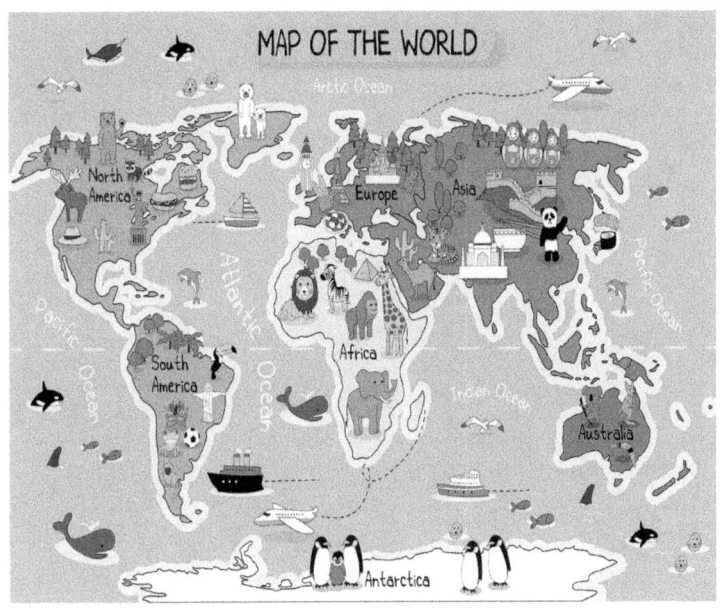